Amelia Bedelia

Unleashed

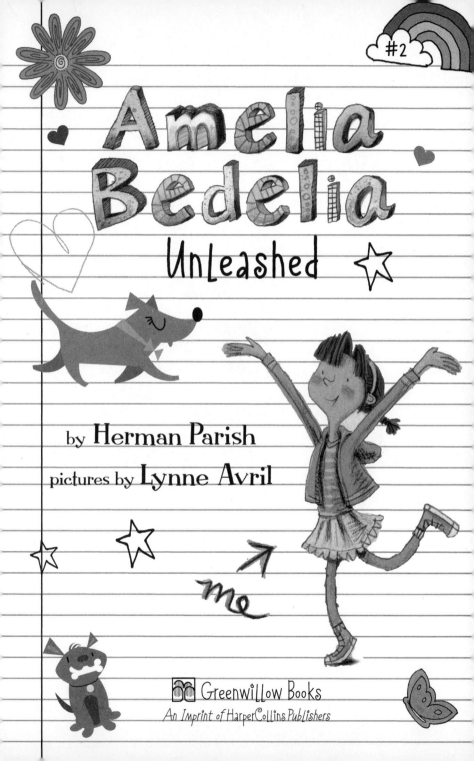

#2

Amelia Bedelia
Unleashed

by Herman Parish

pictures by Lynne Avril

me

Greenwillow Books
An Imprint of HarperCollins Publishers

Amelia Bedelia is a registered trademark of Peppermint Partners, LLC.
Amelia Bedelia Unleashed. Text copyright © 2013 by Herman S. Parish III. Illustrations copyright © 2013 by Lynne
Avril. All rights reserved. No part of this book may be used or reproduced in any manner whatsoever without
written permission except in the case of brief quotations embodied in critical articles and reviews. Printed in the
United States of America. For information address HarperCollins Children's Books, a division of HarperCollins
Publishers, 10 East 53rd Street, New York, NY 10022. www.harpercollinschildrens.com

Library of Congress Cataloging-in-Publication Data is available.

ISBN 978-0-06-209500-8 (hardback)—ISBN 978-0-06-209499-5 (pbk. ed.)
ISBN 978-0-06-227056-6 (pob)

13 14 15 16 17 CG/RRDH 10 9 8 7 6 5 4 3 2 1 First Edition

Greenwillow Books

Larry Lake can spot a Keeper—H.P.

For Chloe, Mr. E.T., and Arthur—L.A.

Contents

Chapter 1: The Big Question 1

Chapter 2: "Have You Seen My Baby?" 8

Chapter 3: A Furry Compromise 17

Chapter 4: A Walk in the Park 29

Chapter 5: Crossing Leashes 37

Chapter 6: "Skate's Up!" 47

Chapter 7: ~~Pup~~ Dog Love 65

Chapter 8: Two-Bit Shave and a Haircut 78

Chapter 9: Dog Gone! 88

Chapter 10: Two for One 100

Chapter 11: Bust into Show 110

Chapter 12: Two Sides Too Many 121

Chapter 13: And Baby Makes Three 130

Chapter 14: Finally . . . the Answer 135

Chapter 1

The Big Question

It certainly seemed like it was going to be another normal evening at Amelia Bedelia's house. Amelia Bedelia's mother was whirling around the kitchen, stirring, boiling, steaming, broiling, and tasting. Supper was almost ready. Something, however, was amiss.

For one thing, Amelia Bedelia's father

1

was sound asleep in his favorite chair. He was usually a big help in the kitchen. But he had looked so tired after work that Amelia Bedelia's mother had suggested he take a little nap. For another thing, the dining room table wasn't set.

"Amelia Bedelia," said her mother, "have you set the table yet?"

Amelia Bedelia glanced up from her homework with a look that said, *Whoops! I forgot!* Then she jumped up to get the silverware.

"Remember the napkins!" her mother called.

"I do!" yelled Amelia Bedelia. "They're dark blue with little white flowers!"

"That's right," her mother said. "Please

remember to put them out for us."

"I'll do that now," said Amelia Bedelia.

"Thanks, sweetie," said her mother. "Do we need glasses?"

"Not yet," said Amelia Bedelia. "Only Dad wears them."

"Right again," said her mother. "I'll get you some water glasses to put out on the table."

"Oh," said Amelia Bedelia. "I already got those glasses."

"Did you fill them?" asked her mother.

"I sure did," said Amelia Bedelia.

Amelia Bedelia's mother peeked at the dining room table. Amelia Bedelia always did just what she was told to do, so every glass was filled right to the brim. Amelia

Bedelia's mother smiled and shook her head.

"Good job, sweetie," she said. "Now please take about a tablespoon of water out of each glass. Otherwise we'll spill and make a mess!"

"Okay," said Amelia Bedelia. She spooned some water out of her parents' glasses. Then she put her lips on the edge of her glass and . . .

SLURP!! SLURP!!

"What's that noise?" called Amelia Bedelia's mother.

"That was me," said Amelia Bedelia. "Who did you think it was?"

"If I didn't know better," said her

4

SLURP!!

mother, "I could have sworn it was a dog drinking out of a bowl."

"I'm glad you didn't swear," said Amelia Bedelia. "You always tell me not to swear. And I'm not a dog."

"So I noticed," said Amelia Bedelia's mother. "But no lady sounds like that when she drinks water."

"I'm not a lady, either," said Amelia Bedelia. "I'm a little girl."

"I noticed that too," said her mom. "But you can at least try to act like a lady, just for practice."

"Why should I ever act like a lady," said Amelia Bedelia, "if I never plan to *be* a lady?"

That news startled her mom so much that she dropped a pot.

Amelia Bedelia's dad leaped up out of his chair, right in the the middle of a snore.

"What was that?" he snorted. Then he ran into the kitchen.

"That was me," said Amelia Bedelia's mother. "Did you enjoy your nap? You woke up just in time for supper." She handed him the salad and a bowl of piping-hot mashed potatoes to take into the dining room. He looked as though he was sleepwalking.

Amelia Bedelia and her mother followed him slowly, carrying the rest of the plates.

As usual, before Amelia Bedelia and her parents began to eat, they said grace. But then, as her parents lifted their full forks to their mouths, Amelia Bedelia asked, "When can we have a baby?"

7

Chapter 2

"Have You Seen My Baby?"

For a few seconds, Amelia Bedelia felt like she was a prisoner in the family photo that her parents enclosed with each Christmas card they sent. But now she was actually alive, while her mom and dad were frozen in time. Their mouths were open. Their forks were right in front of their open mouths. Only their eyes moved, darting back and forth. They looked at each other. They looked at Amelia Bedelia. Amelia Bedelia looked at her mom, then at her dad. Her parents looked back at her, then at each other, then back at her again.

Her parents may not have uttered a word, but their faces were talking at ninety miles an hour. Their eyes grew round, then narrow. Their mouths opened, closed, then opened again. Her parents reminded Amelia Bedelia of the fish she had seen on a class field trip to the aquarium.

Finally Amelia Bedelia could stand it no longer. "What's wrong?" she asked. "You guys look panicked. It's not like I

asked you for something important, like a bigger allowance."

Amelia Bedelia's mother closed her mouth, then opened it again and said, "A baby is much more important than money."

"I was joking," said Amelia Bedelia. "Was I wrong to ask about a baby?"

"No," said her mother. "Not at all."

"We're just a little surprised," said her dad. "Asking for a baby was a bolt out of the blue."

Before Amelia Bedelia could ask him

what nuts and bolts had to do with babies, her mother said, "Is your class at school having lots of babies?"

"Of course not," said Amelia Bedelia. "But the mothers sure are. Last week, Angel became a big sister for the second time. Clay, Roger, and Chip became big brothers this year. Joy has an older brother and now she is getting a little sister. And today my teacher told us that she's going to have a baby this summer."

"How wonderful!" said Amelia Bedelia's mother. "I'm so excited for Mrs. Finley."

"Our whole class is," said Amelia Bedelia. "But I'd like to be excited for *you*. And I want people to be excited for me because I'm going to be a big sister."

"A-*ha!*" said her father. "Now I know what started all this talk about babies."

Amelia Bedelia nodded. "I'd be fine with a boy or a girl—a bolt out of the blue or out of the pink," she said.

Just then Amelia Bedelia's eyes lit up. That's when her mother got really worried. Amelia Bedelia's mother knew that whenever Amelia Bedelia's eyes lit up, real trouble was ahead. As her mother braced herself for what was next, she took a big drink of water.

"I've got it!" announced Amelia Bedelia. "You can have twins—a boy and a girl!"

Her mom sputtered, coughed, and sprayed water all over her plate and the table.

"Gee, Mom," said Amelia Bedelia. "Is that how a lady is supposed to drink water?"

Amelia Bedelia's mother was coughing too much to reply, but she gave Amelia Bedelia a look that told her she was a tiny baby step away from being sent to her room.

Amelia Bedelia's father jumped up and ran over to his wife, patting her on her back to help her breathe.

BING-BONG! went the doorbell.

"Who could that be?" wheezed Amelia Bedelia's mother. "It's dinnertime!"

"Amelia Bedelia," said her dad. "Would you answer the door?"

"What was the question?" said Amelia Bedelia.

Her dad shook his head. "The question is, 'Who is at the door?' Just go see who it is and tell them it's dinnertime."

"Okay," said Amelia Bedelia. "Would

14

BING BONG!!

you like me to invite whoever it is in for supper?"

"No!" said her mom and dad together.

Amelia Bedelia headed for the front door. On her way, she heard her father whisper, "Whew! Saved by the bell!"

How could a bell save someone? Amelia Bedelia wondered. She glanced back at her parents. They were whispering the way she did in class when she tried to pass urgent news to her friends before Mrs. Finley turned around and caught them talking. Now Amelia Bedelia knew how Mrs. Finley felt. She felt like a teacher catching a couple of whisperers.

BING-BONG! BING-BONG! BONG!

Amelia Bedelia's parents looked up

and realized that she had been watching them. Amelia Bedelia pointed at them and said, "You've been saved twice." Then she continued on her way to the front door.

When she got there and peeked out the window, Amelia Bedelia saw a woman pacing back and forth on the front porch. Amelia Bedelia opened the front door.

The woman peered at Amelia Bedelia through the screen door and urgently asked, "Have you seen my baby?"

Chapter 3

A Furry Compromise

"My baby has disappeared!" the lady said.

"When?" said Amelia Bedelia.

"Just a few minutes ago," she said. "I had just given him a bath, clipped his nails, and brushed him. I turned around to get his dinner, and when I turned back—he was gone!"

"This is serious," said Amelia Bedelia. "Come in. You can use our phone to call the police."

"Hah!" said the woman. "They're no help. The last time this happened, they told me to put my baby on a leash. Outrageous!"

Amelia Bedelia couldn't believe her ears. "That's terrible!"

The woman nodded. "I'm glad you agree with me."

"How can I help?" asked Amelia Bedelia.

"Keep your eyes peeled for my baby," said the woman.

"Ouch!" said Amelia Bedelia. That sounded much too painful. She didn't think she could do it, even for a lost baby. She was about to say so when the woman took a stack of papers out of her handbag.

"This is my baby!" she declared. "Isn't he adorable?"

Amelia Bedelia couldn't help herself . . . her mouth opened and her eyes popped out. She hoped that she didn't appear as stunned as she felt. *Yipes,* she thought. *Either that is the ugliest baby I've ever seen, or it's the cutest dog in the world.*

"Well?" the woman said. "Don't you think he's adorable?"

Amelia Bedelia had learned that whenever she didn't know what to say, the best thing to do was to ask a question.

"What's his name?" asked Amelia Bedelia.

"His name is Baby, of course. I took one look at him in the animal shelter and said to myself, *That's my baby*!"

"Oh," said Amelia Bedelia.

"My name is Gladys," said the woman. "Please call this number if you see him."

"My name is Amelia Bedelia," said Amelia Bedelia. "And I will!"

Amelia Bedelia closed the door and went back to the dining room.

"Who was it, sweetie?" asked her mom.

Amelia Bedelia told her parents the story and showed them the picture of Baby.

"You know," said Amelia Bedelia's father, leaning back in his chair. "Having a dog is a lot like having a baby."

Amelia Bedelia and her mom looked at each other, and then back at him, and then back at each other. Then they both burst out laughing.

He ignored them and kept right on talking.

"A dog is a huge responsibility," he said. "You have to love it, feed it, take care of it, and play with it, just like you would a baby."

"But a baby sleeps in a crib," said Amelia Bedelia. "It has toys and pacifiers and teddy bears."

"A dog sleeps in a cozy bed," said her dad. "It has toys, things to chew on, balls to chase."

"Babies cry in the middle of the night," said Amelia Bedelia. "You have to feed them, walk them, pat them, and sing them lullabies."

"You have to walk a dog," said her dad. "They love doggie treats and getting scratched behind their ears. They need shots for rabies and other things."

Amelia Bedelia's mother had heard enough. "Sorry, honey," she said. "I hate to disappoint you, but we are not getting a dog."

Then she folded her arms tightly across her chest. That always meant *No. Absolutely not. No way. Forget it!* "I am putting my foot down," she added.

Amelia Bedelia peeked under the table. Both of her mom's feet were on the floor.

"Why not get a dog?" asked her dad.

"Yeah, why not?" asked Amelia Bedelia.

"Because," said her mom, "if we got a dog, I am the one who would end up having to take care of it!"

"No, you wouldn't," said Amelia Bedelia. "I'll do all the work. I promise! It will be good practice for me before I become a big sister."

BING-BONG! went the doorbell.

This time Amelia Bedelia's mother went to the door. It was Gladys again. Now she was holding a wriggly ball of fur with sparkling eyes. Gladys showed Baby to Amelia Bedelia's mom, who scratched Baby behind his ears as they chatted.

"Can we get a dog, Mom?" asked Amelia Bedelia as Gladys and Baby said good-bye. "Pretty, pretty please?"

Her mother looked at Amelia Bedelia, then at her husband. Then she said, "What kind of dog would you get?"

Yay! thought Amelia Bedelia. This sounded like progress! But it was so sudden, she wasn't sure what to say. So she followed her own rule and asked a question.

"What kinds are there?" she said.

"There are hundreds of breeds," said her father. "There are working dogs, hunting dogs, huge dogs, tiny dogs, dogs that are curly, fuzzy, silky, frizzy. . . ."

"Okay, okay," said Amelia Bedelia.

"To choose the right dog," he said,

"you'll need to do your homework."

"I finished my homework," said Amelia Bedelia. "I can start my dog work as soon as we finish eating."

"Hey," said her mother, "don't you know someone who walks dogs?"

"Diana!" said Amelia Bedelia. "That's perfect. I gave her the idea to start her dog-walking business."

"Well, then," said her mom, "I'm sure she would help you figure out what kind of dog to get."

"Yeah," said her dad. "Maybe you

could help her walk her dogs. You could take different types of dogs for a test drive, like a car, to see which one you liked."

After Amelia Bedelia helped with the dishes, she called Diana. They set a time to meet in the park the next day.

That night, Amelia Bedelia dreamed about dogs and babies. Little babies were perched on top of huge dogs, like jockeys on racehorses. A doorbell rang, and away they went!

BING BONG!!

Chapter 4

A Walk in the Park

The next afternoon, Amelia Bedelia met Diana in the park, just as they had planned. Diana had her dog, Buster, with her. But she was also surrounded by nine other dogs, in all shapes and sizes and colors.

"Hi, Amelia Bedelia! Did you bring any of your famous lemon tarts along with you?" asked Diana.

Amelia Bedelia shook her head. "Sorry, I forgot."

"I'm glad," said Diana. "Those yummy tarts drive my dogs crazy!"

Amelia Bedelia began to scratch a dog behind its long, leathery ears. They were enormous, like an elephant's ears.

"That's a bloodhound. His name is Sherlock," said Diana. "He can follow any trail just by tracking a scent."

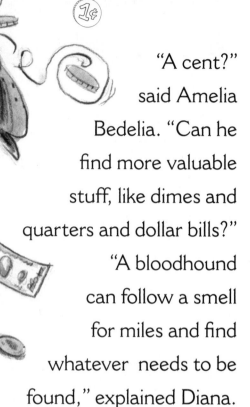

"A cent?" said Amelia Bedelia. "Can he find more valuable stuff, like dimes and quarters and dollar bills?"

"A bloodhound can follow a smell for miles and find whatever needs to be found," explained Diana.

At that moment, all the dogs perked up their ears. Then they all turned their heads in the same direction. Amelia Bedelia and Diana looked too.

Prancing down the path was a magnificent poodle.

"Wow!" said Diana. "What a cutie!"

"Are poodles your favorite dog?" asked Amelia Bedelia.

"That's a terrific poodle," said Diana. "Do you know the boy walking it?"

Amelia Bedelia was so captivated by the dog that she hadn't noticed the boy at all. She looked back at him just as he and his dog came upon a group of skateboarders at the top of the hill.

One of the skateboarders whistled loudly while another bowed deeply. A third yelled, "Hey, dog boy! Who's your girlfriend?" Then they laughed, and they rode in circles around the boy and his dog.

Amelia Bedelia felt bad for him. Those skateboarders went to her school. Tomorrow she would tell them not to be so mean to other people.

"I have a favor to ask," said Diana. "Would you help me return these tired pups to their owners? They are your pals. They won't give you any trouble."

"Sure," said Amelia Bedelia. "I can do that."

"Thanks," said Diana. "I need to get home early. Tonight I'm going on my

very first blind date."
Amelia Bedelia didn't
know what to say, so she
asked a question. "Will you
take his seeing-eye dog for
a walk?"

A curious look came over Diana's
face. Then she began to laugh. "Oh,
honey," she said. "My date isn't blind.
He can see. We've just never met before.
We have friends in common, and they
wanted us to meet since we both work
with dogs. He has a dog-grooming
business and he's a vet."

"Wow!" said Amelia Bedelia. "If Buster
ever gets sick, you can just take him to
your blind date!"

Diana laughed even louder. "No, no, no. He isn't a veterinarian," she said. "He is a *veteran*. He served in the military and worked with dogs. Then he went back to school and learned how to groom dogs. He loves them."

Diana took the leashes of all ten dogs and handed half of them to Amelia Bedelia. "Here you go," she said. "These five live on Maple Street. They're very smart. They'll let you know which house is theirs."

"Thanks for trusting me," said Amelia Bedelia. "And have fun tonight!"

Chapter 5

Crossing Leashes

As Amelia Bedelia headed out of the park toward Maple Street, she ran into the boy and his poodle.

Just to be friendly, Amelia Bedelia said, "Nice dog!"

"Thanks," said the boy. "You've got a lot of nice dogs."

Amelia Bedelia's pack of dogs strained

at their leashes, dragging her over to the poodle. The dogs let out little yips of greeting and approval while they were sniffing and snuffling one another.

Soon their leashes were completely tangled up. They were wrapped every which way around Amelia Bedelia's legs. It looked like some dog maypole dance, with Amelia Bedelia playing the part of the pole.

"I think if I try to move, I'll probably fall over," said Amelia Bedelia, swaying from side to side.

"Then don't move a muscle," said the boy.

He let go of his leash, commanded his poodle to sit (it actually sat), and began to untangle Amelia Bedelia.

"You must love dogs," he said.

"I do," said Amelia Bedelia. "But these aren't mine. I'm helping a friend who walks dogs for a business."

"I should hire your friend," said the boy. "I love my dog, but I hate to walk him. Kids always make fun of me."

"I saw what happened," said Amelia Bedelia. "I know those guys. Tomorrow at school I'll tell them to stop it."

"No! Don't do that,"
said the boy.
"Having a girl
come to my
rescue would
be even worse!"

"But I could
help you," said
Amelia Bedelia.

"Who are you?" said the boy.

"My name is Amelia Bedelia." As soon
as she said it, she could tell by the look on
his face that he'd heard of her.

His eyes lit up, and he said, "Hey, I
remember you. You were on TV. You got in
trouble because of your lemonade stand."

"That's me," said Amelia Bedelia.

"I'm Charlie," said the boy.

"What's your dog's name?" asked Amelia Bedelia.

"This is Pierre," said Charlie.

Charlie motioned for Pierre to come over and sit in front of Amelia Bedelia. Pierre sat up straight and held out his right paw for her to shake.

Amelia Bedelia laughed as she shook Pierre's paw. "What a nice firm paw shake," she said.

Amelia Bedelia wasn't sure what to say next, so she asked a question. "I've never seen such a big poodle. Is Pierre an economy size?"

"He's a standard poodle," said Charlie.

"Gosh," said Amelia Bedelia, "if Pierre is a standard poodle, what does a special poodle look like?"

"Standard is just a size," said Charlie. "It means that he's the biggest type of poodle. It's his fancy haircut that makes him look even more gigantic and kind of silly. It's why I get teased sometimes when I walk him."

"I have a great idea," said Amelia Bedelia. "Meet me here tomorrow. I'll

walk Pierre and you can walk these dogs.
That way no one will tease you."

Amelia Bedelia held out her hand.
Charlie smiled as he took it, shook it, and
said, "It's a deal. See you tomorrow!"

Amelia Bedelia walked
down Maple Street.

The tiny terrier strained
at his leash when he spotted a
jogger running toward
them.

The boxer ran to a
man hitting a punching
bag in his garage.

The bearded collie belonged to a man with a beard.

The husky spotted her owner next.

Last but not least was the sweet Maltese.

Amelia Bedelia had a lot to think about. As she walked home, she wondered about dogs and blind dates and Charlie and Pierre. Most importantly, she wondered what kind of dog was right for her.

Chapter 6

"Skate's Up!"

The next afternoon, Amelia Bedelia's mother looked out the kitchen window. "Uh-oh," she said. "Storm clouds coming. It looks like it's going to rain cats and dogs."

"I hope not," said Amelia Bedelia. "I'd hate to have a Saint Bernard fall on my head. Besides, I have to meet Diana and Charlie in the park."

"Then take this umbrella," said her mother.

Amelia Bedelia shook her head.

"That isn't big enough," she said. "It couldn't save me from a falling Chihuahua."

"Don't worry about that," said Amelia Bedelia's father. "Even if it rains cats and dogs, do you know the worst thing that can happen?"

Years of experience warned Amelia Bedelia not to ask, but she did anyway. "No, Dad," she said. "What's the worst thing that can happen?"

"I'm glad you asked," said her dad. "If

it rains cats and dogs, you might step in a *poodle*." Her father began to chuckle to himself.

Amelia Bedelia shuddered involuntarily at the thought of stepping into Pierre. "That's the worst joke I've ever heard," she said.

Her dad snorted and laughed really loudly. It was so embarrassing. Amelia Bedelia's mother rolled her eyes.

"I hope you realize, honey," she said, "that no one enjoys your jokes more than you do."

Amelia Bedelia arrived at the park on time, even though her mom made her drag along a dumb umbrella. She waited for Diana at the bench where they always met. Charlie and Pierre arrived a few minutes later.

"Hey," said Charlie. "Where are the dogs?"

"I'm not sure," said Amelia Bedelia.

"Diana's late. I'll call her later. I can still walk Pierre for you, if you want me to."

"Okay," said Charlie.

Amelia Bedelia took Pierre's leash, and they began to walk. She told Charlie about her dad's step-in-a-poodle joke. Charlie laughed, and this time she did too.

"Actually," said Charlie, "your dad's

right. A long time ago, poodles were
trained as hunting dogs. They were
retrievers, and they splashed into
ponds and through puddles.
That's how they got their
name."

Amelia Bedelia
couldn't wait
to tell her dad that.

Maybe her dad was smarter than even *he* thought he was.

Up ahead, Amelia Bedelia saw the same bunch of skateboarders Charlie had run into yesterday. They were hanging out right at the top of a long, steep hill. They were exactly where Amelia Bedelia, Charlie, and Pierre were heading.

The skateboarders remembered Pierre and Charlie. They started to laugh and hoot, and the tall one put his fingers to his mouth to whistle, but Amelia Bedelia didn't give him a chance. She did what she did best: she asked a question.

"How do you ride one of these things?"

She hopped onto the deck of a skateboard and wobbled back and forth.

"Whoa!" she yelled, waving her arms
for balance, with an umbrella in one hand
and Pierre's leash in the other.

"It's super easy," said one of the guys.
"Just head downhill and lean from side to
side, like riding a wave on a surfboard."

Suddenly a squirrel bounded by, hop-hop-hopping down the sidewalk. Pierre took off after that squirrel like a rocket. The chase was on!

"Double whoa!" yelled Amelia Bedelia. She squatted down to keep her balance as Pierre pulled her behind him.

Pierre may have looked slightly silly with his groomed and puffy coat, but under those fluffy pom-poms were strong, rippling muscles. He pulled Amelia Bedelia along with no trouble at all. The squirrel raced ahead. Pierre, barking happily, chased the squirrel, and zipping behind them was Amelia Bedelia.

Stop!

Stop!

"Stop, stop, please *ssssttttooooppp*!!!" she hollered, all the way down the hill.

The long, steep sidewalk ended at a large circular fountain, with a round pool that was deep enough for wading. In the center was a statue of a mermaid that spit water into the sky. The mermaid reminded Amelia Bedelia of her mom spitting out her water at the dinner table. Even though she was scared, Amelia Bedelia began to giggle. Then she stopped.

Amelia Bedelia was going so fast she couldn't jump off. She wished her mom could help her now. If she fell, she'd be one giant scab. She wished she'd asked that skateboarder another question: "How do you stop?"

SSsssstttoopp!

The squirrel zigzagged furiously but kept heading for the fountain, with Pierre hot on his trail and Amelia Bedelia holding on for dear life. She leaned backward, forward, from side to side, twisting and turning to keep her balance.

Amelia Bedelia heard shouting. She looked over her shoulder and saw Charlie. He was leading the pack of skateboarders, who were cheering her on.

"Look at her!"

"She's carving like an expert!"

"What a natural!"

"She'll get hurt!" yelled Charlie.

Just then the squirrel darted to the left.

So did Pierre, yanking the leash out of
Amelia Bedelia's hand. Now she was
heading straight for the fountain. Amelia
Bedelia leaned back. *POP!* went her
umbrella as it opened behind her and
began to slow her down. The front wheel
of the skateboard jumped up onto the rim
of the fountain. The spitting mermaid
was the last thing Amelia Bedelia saw
before she shut her eyes.

Charlie and the skateboarders saw
the front end of the skateboard just clear
the edge of the fountain. Amelia Bedelia
leaned forward, toward the mermaid
statue, to catch her balance. Then she

leaned backward as far as she could. She rode the rim of the fountain in a complete, perfect circle. By the time she came around to where she had started, the skateboard had run out of steam. Amelia Bedelia jumped to the ground.

The skateboarders and Charlie stood in stunned silence. Then they all let out a huge whoop and raced toward her.

Charlie was the first to reach Amelia Bedelia. "Are you all right?" he asked.

"I guess so . . . yup!" she said.

The skateboarders went wild. They hoisted Amelia Bedelia onto their shoulders and carried her around and around the fountain.

"You're amazing!"

"What a set of moves!"

"How did you do that?"

"Teach us how to ride like that, like, now!"

Amelia Bedelia laughed. "Okay, but maybe some other day," she said.

"We won't put you down until you promise," said the guys.

"I promise!" said Amelia Bedelia. But then she panicked. "Where is Pierre?"

Charlie pointed at a tree. Pierre was leaping up on the trunk and barking. From a high branch, a chattering squirrel hurled nuts at Pierre's head. Amelia Bedelia and Charlie ran over and grabbed Pierre's leash.

"That was cool, Amelia Bedelia," said Charlie. "It was amazing that you hung on to Pierre's leash. Thanks!"

"No problem," said Amelia Bedelia.

"I know," said Charlie. "Let's go to Pete's Diner to celebrate. Today you can get two hot fudge sundaes for the price of one."

"Great!" said Amelia Bedelia. She hoped her knees would stop shaking by the time they got there.

Amelia Bedelia and Charlie spent the rest of the afternoon at Pete's. Charlie told her all about Pierre and poodles. Amelia Bedelia learned that Charlie's mom was passionate about poodles, but that Pierre was Charlie's responsibility. He fed Pierre and walked Pierre and even groomed and bathed Pierre.

"My mom thinks I do a great job," Charlie said. "She even entered Pierre in that big dog show on Saturday night. She's sure we'll win first prize!"

"You will!" said Amelia Bedelia. "Pierre is amazing."

BA-BOOM! went a clap of thunder. It began to rain cats and dogs. Poor Pierre was outside, getting soaked. Amelia Bedelia pleaded with Pete until he let Pierre come inside, just this once. Charlie parked Pierre under the table in their booth.

"Keep him quiet and out of the way," said Pete. "I don't want anyone to step in a poodle."

From under their table, Pierre let out a huge yawn. It was a long time before Amelia Bedelia and Charlie could stop giggling.

Chapter 7

~~Dog~~ Puppy Love

The very next day, Amelia Bedelia was riding her bike near town when she heard someone call her name.

"Amelia Bedelia! Over here!"

Diana had ten dogs attached to one long leash. She was heading to the park, so Amelia Bedelia rode along beside her.

"I'm so glad to see you," said Amelia

Bedelia. "Was your blind date fun?"

"It was perfect," said Diana. "His name is Eric and he adores dogs. I've been taking all of the dogs I walk to him for grooming. Just look at what a wonderful job he does!"

Amelia Bedelia agreed that the dogs had never looked better or happier. They looked as though they felt important.

"Anything new with you?" asked Diana.

"Lots," said Amelia Bedelia. She told her all about Pierre, skateboarding, and her afternoon at Pete's Diner with Charlie.

"What an adventure," said Diana. "And a little puppy love never hurt anyone."

"Pierre is not a little puppy!" said Amelia Bedelia. "He's a big dog!"

When they got to the park, Amelia Bedelia begged to walk the dogs for Diana.

"Please?" said Amelia Bedelia. "I need to decide what kind I want."

"Thanks!" said Diana, handing her the leash. "These pups are pussy cats, but be alert."

Before Amelia Bedelia could ask how dogs could be cats, Charlie appeared with Pierre. Amelia Bedelia introduced him to Diana. Then they headed off. There were no skateboarders, but plenty of squirrels, so Charlie hung on to Pierre and Amelia Bedelia watched her pack like a hawk.

"Your dogs look great!" said Charlie.

"Don't they?" said Amelia Bedelia. "Diana has them groomed."

They walked on, but Amelia Bedelia could tell that something was bothering Charlie, because he kept fidgeting. Finally she asked, "What's wrong? Are you worried about something?"

"I am," Charlie said. "I'm super nervous about the dog show on Saturday night.

I want Pierre to look perfect."

"Hey," said Amelia Bedelia. "Maybe Diana's friend Eric can groom Pierre too!"

"Thanks," said Charlie. "But my mom wants me to do it."

"Okay," said Amelia Bedelia. "Can I help you, though?"

"Well," said Charlie, "I need to give Pierre a bath on Saturday morning. It's easier with two people, and my mom is super busy. Would you be able to help me?"

"Sure!" said Amelia Bedelia. "I need to ask my parents first, but I'm sure they'll let me. I'll call you!"

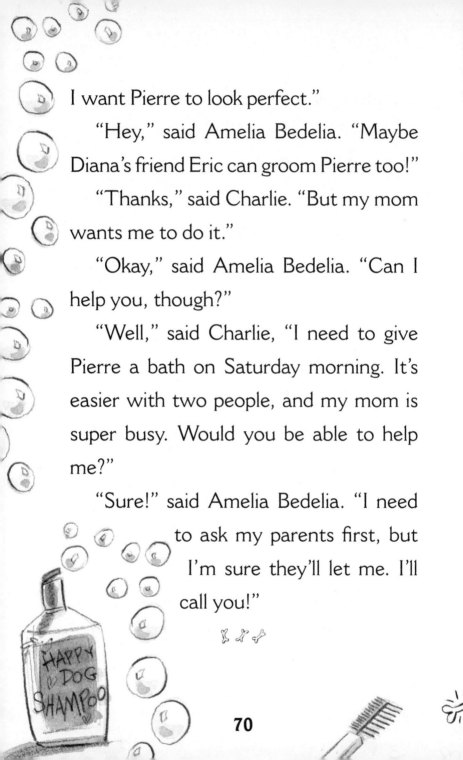

After Charlie and Pierre headed home, Amelia Bedelia decided to give the dogs an extra-long walk. She was exhausted by the time she got them back to Diana. She was way too tired to ride her bike all the way home. She called her father and asked him to come and pick her up.

When her dad arrived, he put her bike in the trunk, while she reclined her seat, let out an enormous yawn, and shut her eyes.

"You're exhausted," said her dad. "Are you dog-tired, or just tired of dogs?"

"Both," she said. "Today was a real drag."

"You didn't have fun?" he said.

"Oh, I had fun," said Amelia Bedelia.

"But with ten dogs, I was the one who got walked. They dragged me here and dragged me there. It was just one long drag."

Amelia Bedelia's dad laughed. "Ten dogs!" he said, "What kind were they?"

Amelia Bedelia counted them off.

"There was
    a Belgian sheepdog,

 an Irish setter,

a German shepherd,

a Scottish terrier,

 a Norwegian elkhound,

 an Italian hound,

and a Welsh corgi."

 "What a group," said her dad. "It sounds like you took most of Europe for a walk."

"Wait a second," said Amelia Bedelia. "I forgot all about the Dane."

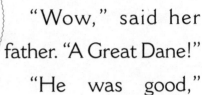

"Wow," said her father. "A Great Dane!"

"He was good," said Amelia Bedelia. "Not really *great*. He misbehaves a lot. Diana says that he eats as much as a lion cub."

"Did you have any trouble, besides the dragging?" asked her dad.

"A little," said Amelia Bedelia. "I let two dogs play, and I lost sight of them for a couple of minutes."

"Did you spot them?" he asked.

"One was already spotted," said Amelia Bedelia. "That was the Dalmatian."

"What was the other one?" asked her dad.

"A Labrador," said
Amelia Bedelia.

"Retriever?" asked her dad.

"Yup," said Amelia Bedelia.
"I found her."

Amelia Bedelia rolled down her window.
She hung her head out to let the cool wind
blow through her hair. She liked the sound
it made as it swirled past her ears.

"*Mmmmmm,*" she said. "I see why
dogs love to do this."

"Wait a second," said her dad. "You're
not turning into a dog, are you? Maybe
you've been hanging out with them too
much. Instead of that necklace you want
for your birthday, we might give you a
flea collar instead."

"Oh, Daddy!" said Amelia Bedelia as they drove in to their driveway.

When they got inside, she told her mother about her day and about Charlie and his poodle, Pierre.

"I adore poodles," said Amelia Bedelia's mother. "Is Pierre a cute little toy poodle?"

"Mom . . . !" said Amelia Bedelia. "He is a real dog. He doesn't need batteries at all."

Then Amelia Bedelia remembered to tell her parents what Charlie had said about poodles and how they got their name from puddles.

"Aha!" said her father. "That's what

we call 'truth in jest.' But what I want to know is . . . did Charlie laugh at my joke about stepping in a poodle?"

"A lot," said Amelia Bedelia.

"This Charlie kid is obviously a genius," said her dad.

After that, it was easy for Amelia Bedelia to get permission to go over to Charlie's house

"You know what?" said her dad. "Your mom and I would love to see the dog show too. We haven't been in years."

"You bet!" said her mom. "It's a plan!"

Chapter 8

Two-Bit Shave and a Haircut

The next day was Saturday, the day of the dog show. Amelia Bedelia rode her bike over to Charlie's house. She was excited to help Charlie give Pierre a bath.

"Charlie," said his mother, "since Amelia Bedelia is here to help you, I'm going to run some quick errands. I'll get Pierre's bath ready for you before I go."

Soon Pierre was standing in a deep tub full of warm water and suds. Amelia Bedelia and Charlie rolled up their sleeves and scrubbed Pierre in the soapy water. Pierre loved getting shampooed. And Amelia Bedelia and Charlie managed to stay pretty dry until it was time to dry Pierre.

Both Amelia Bedelia and Charlie could see it coming. It was like those weather maps on TV that show an approaching hurricane. They were in the storm's path and were going to get soaked. Sure enough, Pierre let them have it. After one second of shaking, they were drenched.

The only thing they could do was

holler and shriek and dance around and
laugh. A lot.

"Charlie!" yelled Amelia Bedelia. "You
look like you just ran through one hundred
sprinklers for an hour!"

"You look like you fell into the world's biggest swimming pool!" yelled Charlie.

Then, starting with his head and moving down to his rear end, Pierre shook himself one last time, just to be sure they were *totally* soaked.

Still laughing, Amelia Bedelia and Charlie led Pierre out to the back deck. They worked in the sunshine, squirting conditioner into Pierre's coat and rubbing it in with their fingers.

"Let's start brushing him," said Charlie.

"Fun!" said Amelia Bedelia. She grabbed a nearby brush from a dustpan. When she began to brush Pierre with it, Charlie laughed.

"Not that kind of brush!" he said.
"You'll get him dirty again. Use one of
these special dog brushes."

Amelia Bedelia loved brushing Pierre.
"He's going to be beautiful!" she said.

"You mean handsome," said Charlie.

82

Once Pierre's hair was tangle free, Charlie showed Amelia Bedelia how to trim his coat with the electric clippers. Charlie was trimming stray hairs from Pierre's fluffy chest when disaster struck. A squirrel ran across the deck. Pierre took off after him like a shot! He ran right over Charlie, who was still holding the whirring clippers.

Charlie hit the deck.

"No, Pierre!" he shouted. "Heel! Wait! Come back! If you get dirty, you'll have to take another bath!"

Pierre was an obedient dog, and besides, the squirrel had already scrambled

up a tree. Pierre trotted back to
Charlie and sat down again.

That's when Amelia Bedelia
noticed a long strip of fluffy white
fur on the deck.

"Hey, Charlie,
where did this
come from?"
she asked.

There was only
one place it could
have come from: Pierre's
beautiful prize-winning coat.

Charlie kneeled in front of Pierre.
"Uh-oh," he said.

It looked as though a lawnmower

had cut a swath through a pretty flower bed.

"Oh boy," said Charlie. "Boy, oh boy, oh boy. This is not good. Not good at all."

He took the fluffy patch of hair from Amelia Bedelia and tried to push it back into place. It didn't work.

"We need tape or something," said Amelia Bedelia. "Or paste or a glue stick."

They tried everything. Nothing worked.

"Boy, oh boy," said Charlie. "I am doomed."

Pierre sat patiently. Perhaps he realized that he was partly to blame. But now, as he watched a puff of fur that used to be

his beautiful pom-pom blow across the deck like a tiny tumbleweed, the situation began to sink in to him too.

Amelia Bedelia thought that if ever an animal were going to speak, it would be now.

Pierre cocked his head and stared directly at them. His eyes said, "You've *got* to be kidding me. I trusted you to take care of me, and *this* happens. *Woof!*"

Charlie started pacing back and forth across the deck, repeating "Boy, oh boy" and tugging at his own hair.

"I know," said Amelia Bedelia, "let's

look in the kitchen. There's probably something there that would work."

They searched through kitchen drawers until Amelia Bedelia found some twisty ties. She headed back to the deck to try them on Pierre, while Charlie kept looking for possible solutions.

"Charlie!" yelled Amelia Bedelia. "Your problem is gone!"

"Great!" Charlie called back. "Do the twisty ties work?"

"I don't know," said Amelia Bedelia. "Pierre is gone—vanished!"

Dog Gone!

Charlie dashed out to the deck. "Pierre, Pierre!" he called. "Come here, boy! Come here, Pierre!"

Amelia Bedelia could hear the panic in Charlie's voice. They kept calling and calling Pierre's name, over and over, until it seemed to echo through the entire neighborhood. But it was no use. Pierre had evaporated into thin air.

Pierre?

"This is all my fault," said Charlie. "Pierre probably feels stupid, like I do, and he's run away."

"I know," said Amelia Bedelia. "Let's make posters and hang them up in the neighborhood. That worked for a lady I know who lost her dog, Baby."

"We don't have time," said Charlie. "This is an emergency! I am cooked. The dog show is in a couple of hours! Mom is depending on me."

Amelia Bedelia watched the breeze blow another tuft of Pierre's fur across the deck. She caught it and held it to her nose. She could still smell the yummy conditioner they had used. Her eyes grew large, and she said, "Charlie, I'm pretty sure you're not cooked. I've got a real idea. But I need to call someone before I tell you what it is."

Charlie handed her a phone. This is what he heard Amelia Bedelia say:

"Hi, Diana? It's me, Amelia Bedelia. Hi. I'm okay. You know that bloodhound

you walk? Sherlock . . . right, like the detective. Can I take him for a walk today? . . . Like right now . . . Perfect! Will you tell Mr. Holm I'm picking him up? Thanks! We're on our way."

Amelia Bedelia grabbed Charlie's hand. "Let's go!" she said. "Sherlock is on the case, and he'll help us for sure!"

"Those are the droopiest jowls I've ever seen!" said Charlie. They were headed back to the deck, the last place they had seen Pierre.

"Sherlock can find anything," said Amelia Bedelia. "We just need to give him a clue to work with."

She waved the tuft of Pierre's fur

under Sherlock's nose. His tail began to wag from side to side, faster and faster.

"Bah-ROOO!" bayed Sherlock. He took off, dragging Amelia Bedelia and Charlie along behind him.

"Bah-ROOO! Bay-ROOO!"

They ran over lawns, through backyards, across a tennis court, then straight down a street lined with stores. Sherlock led them right into the nearest butcher shop!

"We're wasting time," moaned Charlie. "Sherlock doesn't know where Pierre is. He just wants lunch."

Amelia Bedelia wasn't so sure.

"Excuse me," she said to the butcher. "Did a huge French poodle stop by here?"

The butcher laughed. "You mean the dog with the world's worst haircut?"

"Wow! That's him," said Charlie.

"Yeah," said the butcher. "He was here a few minutes ago. He looked miserable. Hey, who butchered his hair?"

Amelia Bedelia and Charlie looked at each other.

"Anyway," said the butcher, "I felt sorry for him, so I gave him a hot dog."

"That was really nice of you," said Amelia Bedelia.

"Here," said the butcher. "Here's a hot dog for your bloodhound."

"Thank you," said Amelia Bedelia. "This can be a special treat for Sherlock when he finds Pierre."

"*If* he finds Pierre," said Charlie.

Amelia Bedelia dangled the tuft of Pierre's hair under Sherlock's nose once more. "Track!" she said.

"*Bah-ROOO! Bay-ROOO!*" bayed Sherlock, and away they went. Amelia Bedelia could tell that Sherlock was hot on Pierre's trail. They bounded through

Bah-Rooo!

backyards, over a compost heap, into a briar patch, and across a stream, where Sherlock paused to sniff the bank. Amelia Bedelia looked at Charlie. "You're a total mess," she said.

"So are you," said Charlie. "If we look this bad, imagine what Pierre is going to look like. Kiss the dog show good-bye."

"Bay-roooooo!" bayed Sherlock at the top of his lungs. This time, there was a reply. They heard a feeble *woof* that sounded as though it was coming from miles away.

"It's Pierre!" Charlie shouted.

Sherlock took off again, and led them to a culvert, a tunnel that let the stream flow under a road. There they found

Bay-Rooo!

Pierre. He was a wet, cold, shivering, dirty, disgusting mess. Still, they both threw their arms around him. He covered their faces with kisses in return.

Amelia Bedelia hugged Sherlock and gave him his hot-dog treat. It disappeared into his jowls and was devoured in one gulp. *"Bahhhhh!"*

"I think he's saying thank you!" said Amelia Bedelia, laughing.

Amelia Bedelia and Charlie returned Sherlock to Mr. Holm on their way back to Charlie's house. Charlie's mom drove in to the driveway just as they lifted Pierre into the warm, soapy bath. When she checked on their progress, she was surprised to find Pierre still in the tub.

"My goodness," she said. "You two are going to wash him away!"

"I just want him to look his best," said Charlie. That wasn't really a lie, thought Amelia Bedelia, but it wasn't the whole truth either. She concluded that it was just a fib.

"Well, shout if you need me," said Charlie's mom. "I'll be down in my office."

While Charlie scrubbed the muck out of Pierre's coat and pulled out burrs and briars, Amelia Bedelia called Diana again. This is what she said:

"Can your friend Eric, the dog groomer, perform miracles?"

Chapter 10

Two for One

Diana and Eric arrived at Charlie's house in Eric's mobile dog-grooming van. Painted on the side of the van was a sign that said WOOF-WOOF GROOMER. There was also a giant picture of the head of a happy, barking dog, with the words "Woof-woof!" coming out of its mouth. Underneath the picture was Eric's business slogan: "The groomer dogs ask for by name!"

Diana introduced Eric to Amelia Bedelia and Charlie. Then they led Pierre, who was wrapped up in towels, through the back door of the van and hoisted him onto the grooming table.

"Okeydokey," said Eric. "Let's see what we're up against." Charlie slowly peeled the towels off Pierre. Eric let out a low whistle. He walked around Pierre four times. Then Eric shook his head, looked at Charlie, and asked, "You did this?"

Charlie nodded.

"Man," asked Eric, "what did you use for clippers, a weed whacker?"

"Eric, these kids feel bad enough," said Diana. "Can you help them out?"

Eric shrugged. "I don't know, guys. Only time can repair this. In a couple of months, when his hair grows back, I'll come over and clip him right."

"But . . . but . . . ," said Amelia Bedelia, "the dog show is tonight!"

"I really wish I could help," said Eric. "But see for yourself. One side is perfect and the other side is a train wreck. I'm just a groomer, not a magician."

"There's nothing you can do?" asked Diana.

"Well," said Eric. "You'd have to rethink this dog. Completely."

"Pierre is a poodle," said Charlie. "Thinking isn't going to change that."

"My dad always says that there are two sides to everything," said Amelia Bedelia. "Pierre definitely has two sides. Can you make the best of each side?"

"Hmmm," said Eric. "You might be on to something, Amelia Bedelia." He walked around Pierre again and said, "If we keep this one side like a perfect show poodle, but make the other something really fun, well . . ."

"That could look cool," said Diana.

"What do you think, Charlie?" asked Amelia Bedelia. "After all, Pierre is your dog."

Charlie shrugged. "Well, Pierre doesn't stand a chance of winning anything now," he said. "So I guess it's worth a shot."

Eric smiled. "After I finish," he said, "you'll have the most amazing dog in town."

Eric went right to work. He carefully groomed the poodle side until it was absolutely perfect and fluffy and pouffy. Then he began to trim the other side. He clipped and hummed and fluffed and puffed and tweaked and twirled. Amelia Bedelia thought Eric looked like a famous artist creating a masterpiece. She thought Pierre was smiling too.

"Well?" said Eric finally. "What do you think?"

Amelia Bedelia, Diana, and Charlie studied Pierre. They all agreed that he looked interesting . . . but something was missing.

"It needs to be even more dramatic," said Eric. "Dramatically different."

"You know," said Diana, "I once saw a dancer who had a fabulous costume. One side was a fancy white dress and he looked like a woman, but when he turned, the other side was a fancy black tuxedo, and he looked like a man. When he danced, he played both parts. I'll never forget it."

Eric was nodding again. "Yes . . . fancy black, fancy white!"

Then he turned and asked, "How do you guys feel about dyeing?"

"I really don't want to," said Amelia Bedelia. "I'm way too young."

"I might as well," said Charlie. "My mom is going to kill me anyway when she sees Pierre."

Diana smiled. "Eric means dyeing something another color," she said.

"Charlie," said Eric, "would you mind if I dyed Pierre's wild side black?"

"Go for it," said Charlie.

"I've got nothing to lose."

Amelia Bedelia nodded. She liked the way Charlie thought about things and how flexible he was.

Diana and Eric whipped up some black dye in the sink in the van. "Don't worry, this is a vegetable dye," Eric said. "It will wash out in a few days."

Amelia Bedelia, Charlie, and Diana watched as Eric brushed on the dye. Pierre stamped his feet once or twice, but otherwise he seemed to like the feel of the dye brush. When Eric stepped back from the table, they were all quiet.

"Wow," said Charlie finally. "Pierre looks amazing."

"Bravo, Eric!" said Diana as she gave him

a hug. "Pierre looks fantastic."

"He sure does," said Amelia Bedelia.
"He's two dogs in one."

Chapter 11

Bust into Show

There was a dog show every year in Amelia Bedelia's town, and at first it seemed as though this one was going to be like all the rest. Dog owners were whirling around backstage, combing, brushing, fussing, primping, and preening until their dogs were ready for their moment in the spotlight. Spectators, friends, and

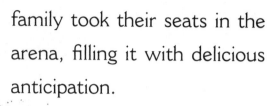

family took their seats in the arena, filling it with delicious anticipation.

Something, however, was wrong. It was Pierre. Amelia Bedelia and Charlie had snuck Pierre into his dog carrier and into the car. Luckily Charlie's mom hadn't noticed his new look. Unluckily they had dropped the crate on Charlie's foot. And now they had to sneak Pierre into the show. They didn't want him to be disqualified before it even started.

"I picked up tickets for Amelia Bedelia's parents," said Charlie's mom, "so I'll go join them. We will see you both after the

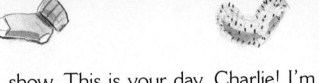

show. This is your day, Charlie! I'm sure you'll knock everyone's socks off."

Amelia Bedelia imagined the arena filled with flying socks, raining down on Pierre and Charlie as the crowd cheered.

"Okay. Bye, Mom," said Charlie. He opened his eyes wide and gave Amelia Bedelia a panicked look.

Normally, you don't have to sneak a prize-winning poodle into a dog show. How were they ever going to get Pierre out of his crate, past all the other dogs and owners and handlers and judges, without anyone noticing that half of him was a fluffy white purebred champion poodle, and the other half was a mascot for a motorcycle gang?

Charlie kneeled down to open the door of the crate and winced as he leaned on his foot. "I'm just going to walk Pierre to his spot and hope no one is looking," he said to Amelia Bedelia. "Is the coast clear?"

A puzzled look came over Amelia Bedelia's face. "Is the coast clear?" she repeated. "How would I know what the weather is at the beach? All I know is that everyone seems to be watching us."

"This will never work," Charlie said. "Plus, my foot is killing me."

"Hey, you two!" a voice boomed.

Charlie and Amelia Bedelia froze. Then they slowly turned around.

"How are you guys?" asked Diana.

"Whew!" said Amelia Bedelia. "You gave us twin freak-outs. I thought you were coming to arrest us."

"We came to wish you good luck," said Diana.

"Do you need help?" asked Eric.

"We sure do," said Charlie. He pointed at a spot across the room. "We need to get Pierre way over there without anyone seeing him."

"Gotcha," said Eric. "You want to get the dog out of the box without letting the cat out of the bag."

That utterly confused Amelia Bedelia, but Charlie said, "Exactly!" So she figured it must be all right.

"Okay," said Eric. "One step at a time. Here we go."

"Come, Pierre," said Charlie, limping as he led Pierre out of the crate.

Diana and Eric walked next to Pierre on one side, and Amelia Bedelia and Charlie walked next to Pierre on the other side.

"Fun! It's a Pierre sandwich!" said Amelia Bedelia.

Once they had finally crossed the crowded room, Charlie pointed to the spot reserved for them, and Pierre lay

down with his perfect-poodle side up.

"Amazing," said Eric with a laugh. "If I didn't know better, I'd never guess that Pierre had a wild side."

"Pierre is the best," said Amelia Bedelia.

"Charlie," asked Diana, "are you going to be the handler for Pierre?"

"I usually am," said Charlie. "But my

foot still really hurts. I'm sure it will be okay in a minute, but . . . would you be his handler?"

"Well," said Diana, "how about Amelia Bedelia? Pierre knows and trusts her."

"Great!" said Charlie. "That sounds good to me."

"That sounds crazy to me," said Amelia Bedelia. "I've never shown a dog in my life!"

"You'll be terrific," said Diana. "It's simple. Just do whatever the judges tell you and Pierre to do."

Just then the announcer called for Pierre's group. Charlie touched up Pierre's perfect-poodle side with a brush. He touched up Pierre's wonderful wild side with a comb and some spit. Amelia Bedelia looked more nervous than Pierre.

"Would you like me to comb your hair too?" asked Charlie.

Amelia Bedelia looked at the spitty comb. "No, thank you!" she said, giggling.

"We'll be cheering in the stands," said Eric.

"Good luck," Diana said. "Have fun!"

Before she knew what had happened, Amelia Bedelia was in line with the other dogs and handlers. She realized that she knew most of them. Sherlock was there. So were the jogger and her Jack Russell terrier, and the Maltese and her owner. Even Gladys was there, cradling Baby in her arms.

"Congratulations!" Gladys said. "You finally got your dog!"

"Not yet," said Amelia Bedelia. "I'm here helping a friend."

"Good luck," said Gladys as she put Baby down. "May the best dog win."

"Ladies and gentlemen," said the announcer, "we proudly present our final group of the evening."

Pierre looked up at Amelia Bedelia. She looked down at him. He wagged his tail twice. Then the lights dimmed in the arena, the spotlight came on, the curtain parted, and Amelia Bedelia and Pierre bounded out to face the judges.

Chapter 12

Two Sides Too Many

First off, the judges had all the dogs run in a line in the same direction to examine how well they moved. This showed off Pierre's perfect-poodle side beautifully. The judges looked pleased. The crowd roared its approval. *I can do this*, thought Amelia Bedelia. *I am doing this*.

Announcers named Bob and Melanie

described the action for the fans. Their voices filled the arena.

Bob: "Melanie, this last group of dogs is what we've all been waiting for—they're the cream of the crop!"

Melanie: "That's right, Bob. Any dog here could easily take home the trophy."

Bob: "Look at the bloodhound. I'd hate to have him on my trail."

Melanie: "That tiny Maltese is a gem! I wish my hair looked that good, Bob."

Bob: "We all do, Melanie. What a cutie!"

Melanie: "Sherlock is being followed by the Jack Russell terrier, another favorite with the crowd."

Bob: "Listen to that applause. That's a little dog with tons of personality."

Melanie: "Here comes another star—Pierre, the French standard poodle. I remember him from last year."

Bob: "There's nothing standard about Pierre. He towers over that tiny Yorkshire terrier."

Melanie: "That Yorkie is Baby. Adorable."

Bob: "Now the judges are having them reverse direction, showing off the other side of these champions to this very enthusiastic crowd."

The audience began to applaud again. But gradually, the applause petered out. The crowd buzzed. Something was different. Something was wrong.

Up in the stands, Charlie's mom appeared to be the most perplexed of all. She looked at Amelia Bedelia's parents. "Where's Pierre?" she asked.

"I can see Amelia Bedelia," said Amelia Bedelia's father, "but I still can't see Pierre. I must need new glasses."

"I see Amelia Bedelia too," said her mom. "But I can't see Pierre, either.

I must finally need glasses."

"No, you don't," said Charlie's mom. She was looking through binoculars. "Your eyes are fine. Pierre has been replaced by a big black dog!"

Melanie: "Bob, the judges are confused."

Bob: "So am I, Melanie."

Melanie: "Now the judges are conferring . . . scratching their heads . . . shaking their heads. They're counting. Looks like one is missing."

Bob: "A judge is missing?"

Melanie: "No, Bob, a *dog*. A dog is missing."

Bob: "Good grief! It appears Pierre the poodle has vanished! He's been replaced by a large black dog."

Melanie: "Let's see what the judges do, Bob."

This is what the judges did. They directed Amelia Bedelia to walk back and forth, to and fro. The crowd gasped, then fell totally silent. Amelia Bedelia smiled and patted Pierre on the head.

At first Amelia Bedelia's parents didn't know what to think. When their daughter turned the poodle one way, he was white and fluffy. When she turned him the other way, he was black and curly.

"Oh," said Amelia Bedelia's father. "I get it. One side is a standard poodle, and the other side is a poodle that has been stepped in."

P-Air! P-Air!

Amelia Bedelia's mother laughed harder than she had ever laughed in her life.

"At last," her father said, "you laughed at one of my jokes."

"Pierre, my man, you rock!" yelled Eric. He jumped up and began to clap and chant Pierre's name: "P-Air! P-Air! P-Air!"

"P-Air! P-Air! P-Air! P-Air!" shouted Amelia Bedelia's parents.

"P-Air! P-Air!" shouted Charlie's mother.

"P-Air! P-Air! P-Air! P-Air! P-Air! P-Air! P-Air! P-Air!" chanted the crowd.

Amelia Bedelia could see Charlie peeking out from behind the curtain. She

P-Air! P-Air! P-Air! P-Air!

beckoned him to come and join her, and when he did Pierre jumped up and licked his face. Then Pierre wagged his tail and wouldn't stop wagging. The crowd cheered, chanting even louder.

"P-Air! P-Air! P-Air! P-Air! P-Air! P-Air! P-Air! P-Air!"

Chapter 13

And Baby Makes Three

Finally the cheers of the crowd died down enough for the judges to hear themselves talk. And talk they did. Their tongues were wagging faster than Pierre's tail. At last the judges reached a decision.

The head judge spoke into a microphone, and his voice boomed across the arena. "In the history of this dog show, we have never had a situation so unusual or a dog as unusual as Pierre."

The crowd cheered. Hooray! Yay!

"As remarkable as Pierre's appearance is, it is against the rules of the show to change the natural color of a dog's coat, even half of it. That is why we have disqualified Pierre the poodle." Boo!

The crowd booed. Boo!

"However, it is our decision that such an unusual presentation deserves some unusual recognition. Therefore, we are giving Pierre a special award for Most Original Grooming."

The crowd applauded loudly as the judges shook hands with Charlie and Amelia Bedelia. When Pierre offered them his paw, each judge shook it and bowed. The crowd roared its approval.

Baby won Best in Show. Amelia Bedelia felt fine about that, since she thought Baby was the cutest dog in the world and had thought that since the first time she laid eyes on him.

Baby may have been awarded the trophy, but there was no doubt who the true star was. Pierre was mobbed after the show. Amelia Bedelia and Charlie took turns having their pictures taken with Pierre and his fans. And since Pierre had two sides, everyone wanted two pictures. Cameras and phones flashed and clicked and snapped until you'd have thought a movie star had moved to town.

"You know, Charlie," said Amelia Bedelia's dad after everyone had been introduced officially. "They say every dog has his day."

"I've heard that," said Charlie.

"Well," continued her dad, "even though Pierre didn't win Best in Show, this day and night belongs to Pierre."

"And you too, Charlie," said Amelia Bedelia. "You're both the best!"

"Thanks, Amelia Bedelia," said Charlie. "I think I owe it all to you!"

Everyone was too excited to go home, so they stopped by Pete's Diner for his two-for-one treats and had a little party. Pete let Pierre park under the table again because it was such a special night. He even brought him a bowl filled with water.

SLURP!!

Chapter 14

Finally . . . the Answer

Amelia Bedelia's parents were true to their word. On Sunday afternoon, they all got in the car to go get a dog.

"Are we going to the pet store by the mall?" asked Amelia Bedelia.

"No," said her dad, "I thought we'd stop by the animal shelter for a dog. They're by the pound."

"By the pound?" said Amelia Bedelia. "Is that how you buy a dog, like potatoes or butter or something?"

"Of course not," said her mother. "The town pound is where they keep lost or abandoned animals. The adopt-a-pet shelter tries to find them homes."

"That makes more sense," said Amelia Bedelia. "If you bought a Great Dane by the pound, you'd have to be a millionaire."

"They don't sell these dogs at all," said her father. "They give them away."

"For free?" said Amelia Bedelia. "That's a better deal than two-for-one ice cream specials at Pete's Diner."

"Actually," said her dad, "they're not quite free. You have to pay for their shots

and a dog license."

"Daddy, you're always teasing me," said Amelia Bedelia. "Dogs don't need license plates. No dog can run fast enough to get a speeding ticket."

As they pulled up to the shelter, Amelia Bedelia realized something. After all the different kinds of dogs she had seen and walked and cared for, she still had not decided what kind of dog would be best for her. She could hear the dogs barking inside the shelter. She wondered if one was calling to her.

Amelia Bedelia and her parents met the director of the shelter—a lady named Wiggins. She was only too happy to help them.

"I'm retired now," she said. "But I was a vet."

"Were you in the army or navy or air force?" asked Amelia Bedelia.

Dr. Wiggins laughed. "None of the above. I was a veterinarian for thirty years."

"Sweetie," said Amelia Bedelia's mom, "we're going to wait here while you choose. This is your dog. You ought to decide for yourself which one is right for you."

"How will I know?" said Amelia Bedelia as tears began to well up in her eyes.

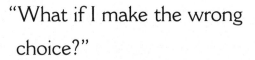 "What if I make the wrong choice?"

"Don't worry, honey," said Dr. Wiggins. "You can trust yourself. You'll feel which one is right for you. I'll help. Now let's go meet some dogs."

As soon as they entered the kennel, the noise became deafening. Dogs of all shapes and sizes and colors wanted Amelia Bedelia's attention. Dogs were barking, yipping, and yapping. They were turning around and around to show themselves off. They were wagging their tails so eagerly Amelia Bedelia thought their tails might fly off their rear ends all at once.

As she walked down the long row of cages, Amelia Bedelia stopped to meet every single dog. All of the dogs acted like they would love to go home with Amelia Bedelia . . . all except one.

This dog was just sitting there, alert but not bouncy, interested but not excited. It was adorable! It tilted its head to one side to look at Amelia Bedelia.

Amelia Bedelia
tilted her head and
looked right back at it.

"I've seen a lot of dogs
lately. But I have never
seen one like that,"
said Amelia Bedelia,
pointing at the dog. "What kind is it?"

"That dog is a mixture," Dr. Wiggins
said.

"A mixture of what?" asked Amelia
Bedelia.

"She's a mixture of her mother and
her father," said Dr. Wiggins.

"Gosh," said Amelia Bedelia. "That
sounds like me."

"You and everyone else in the world,"

said Dr. Wiggins. "We are all mutts, when you come right down to it."

"She's just a mutt?" asked Amelia Bedelia.

"Just a mutt?" asked Dr. Wiggins. "Why, a mutt can be the most wonderful dog in the world. With a mutt like this one, chances are you'll get the best of everything—the courage of a terrier, the friendliness of a spaniel, the brains of a poodle, the affection of a retriever, the loyalty of a hound. All rolled into one."

"Wow," said Amelia Bedelia. "I never thought of it like that."

Dr. Wiggins opened the cage door.

Amelia Bedelia kneeled down to get a
closer look, and the first thing that dog did
was to lick her cheek, just once. Amelia
Bedelia sat back and blinked her eyes,
like Sleeping Beauty being awakened by
a kiss.

"This is the one," said Amelia Bedelia.
"This is the dog for me."

"Good choice," said Dr. Wiggins.
"She's a sweetheart."

"How adorable!" said Amelia Bedelia's mother when Amelia Bedelia and Dr. Wiggins returned to the office with the dog. "You two look like you were made for each other."

"What's her name?" asked Amelia Bedelia's father.

"Finally," said Amelia Bedelia.

"It did take a while," said her mom.

"And it's been quite a saga," said her dad. "But you got a dog at last. What are you going to call her?"

"Finally," said Amelia Bedelia. "I am going to call her Finally Bedelia, because I finally got what I wanted: a dog."

After they had officially adopted Finally, everyone headed back to the car.

Amelia Bedelia's father opened the back door. Finally jumped onto the backseat like she had done it a million times before, and they headed for home.

"Just so you know," said her dad, glancing in the rearview mirror. "We're still working on that baby brother for you."

"Or baby sister," said her mother.

"Take your time," said Amelia Bedelia. "I've got my own baby now."

Amelia Bedelia rolled her window

down. Finally came over to sit on Amelia Bedelia's lap. She poked her head out the window. Amelia Bedelia couldn't wait to introduce her to Charlie, Diana, and Eric. She was sure Finally would be Pierre's best friend.

Amelia Bedelia stuck her head out the window too. The breeze blew Finally's ears back, tickling Amelia Bedelia's face. Her hair mixed with Finally's furry ears until you couldn't tell where Amelia Bedelia ended and Finally began.

The Amelia Bedelia
Chapter Books

Hi!
I'm going on
a road trip next.
Hope I don't fall!

Read these great books about
Amelia Bedelia!

#1

Amelia Bedelia Means Business

by Herman Parish   pictures by Lynne Avril

#2

Amelia Bedelia Unleashed

by Herman Parish   pictures by Lynne Avril

Dear Amelia Bedelia fan,

Usually, this is where you would be able to read the first chapter of Amelia Bedelia's next book, *Amelia Bedelia Road Trip!* But after all her adventures with dogs, we ran out of pages. And the truth is, I haven't written the first chapter yet. However, I have written the *last* chapter. If you read the ending of a story, though, it's usually not as much fun to read the rest of it, so I'm not going to share the last chapter . . . yet.

At this point, Amelia Bedelia would ask a question: How can you write the end of a story before you write the beginning?

Good question. Have you ever tried to write a story that way? You should try it! For *Road Trip!* I knew where Amelia Bedelia would be at the end of the story—she and her parents would wind up back at home. But they wouldn't feel the same as they had when they started. They would have had all kinds of funny, weird, interesting encounters with people they met in the places they went.

That's the part I'm working on right now. I hope you'll have as much fun reading about Amelia Bedelia's adventures on the road as I'm having writing about them!

Keep reading and writing,

Herman Parish

Herman Parish

Two Ways to Say It

By Amelia Bedelia

"She's put her foot down."  "She said no, and she means it."

"It's raining cats and dogs!" "It's pouring!"

"I went on a blind date." "I went on a date with someone I hadn't met before."

"Oh, it's puppy love!" "We are young and we like each other!"

"That's a bolt out of the blue!" "What a surprise!"

"Knock their socks off!" "Surprise them with how great you are!"

"Don't let the cat out of the bag." "Don't ruin the surprise."